Chinese Graded Reader

Level 1: 300 Characters

六十年的夢

Liùshí Nián de Mèng

The Sixty Year Dream

based on *Rip Van Winkle*
by Washington Irving

Mind Spark Press LLC

SHANGHAI

Published by Mind Spark Press LLC

Shanghai, China

Mandarin Companion is a trademark of Mind Spark Press LLC.

Copyright © Mind Spark Press LLC, 2013

For information about educational or bulk purchases, please contact
Mind Spark Press at business@mandarincompanion.com.

Instructor and learner resources and traditional Chinese editions of
the Mandarin Companion series are available
at www.MandarinCompanion.com.

First paperback print edition 2013

Library of Congress Cataloging-in-Publication Data
Irving, Washington.

The Sixty Year Dream : Mandarin Companion Graded Readers: Level 1,
Simplified Chinese Edition / Washington Irving; [edited by] John Pasden, Yang
Renjun, Yu Cui

1st paperback edition.

Shanghai, China / Salt Lake City, UT: Mind Spark Press LLC, 2013

Library of Congress Control Number: 2015901574
ISBN: 9781941875049 (Paperback)
ISBN: 9781941875179 (Paperback/traditional ch)
ISBN: 9780991005215 (ebook)
ISBN: 9780991005291 (ebook/traditional ch)

Mandarin Companion Graded Readers

Now you can read books in Chinese that are fun and help accelerate language learning. Every book in the Mandarin Companion series is carefully written to use characters, words, and grammar that a learner is likely to know.

The Mandarin Companion Leveling System has been meticulously developed through an in-depth analysis of textbooks, education programs and natural Chinese language. Every story is written in a simple style that is fun and easy to understand so you improve with each book.

Mandarin Companion Level 1

Level 1 is intended for Chinese learners at an upper-elementary level. Most learners will be able to approach this book after one to two years of formal study, depending on the learner and program. This series is designed to combine simplicity of characters with an easy-to-understand storyline which helps learners to expand their vocabularies and language comprehension abilities. The more they read, the better they will become at reading and grasping the Chinese language.

Level 1 is based on a core set of 300 fundamental characters, ensuring each book's vocabulary will be simple everyday words that the reader is most likely to know. Level 1 books contain approximately 400 unique words, introducing a limited number of new key words relevant to the story.

Key words are added gradually over the course of the story accompanied by a numbered footnote for each instance. Pinyin and an English definition are provided at the bottom of the page for the first instance of each key word, and a complete glossary is provided at the back of the book. All proper nouns have been underlined to help the reader distinguish between names and other words.

What level is right for me?

If you are able to comfortably read this book without looking up lots of words, then this book is likely at your level. It is ideal to have at most only one unknown word or character for every 40-50 words or characters that are read.

Once you are able to read fluidly and quickly without interruption you are ready for the next level. Even if you are able to understand all of the words in the book, we recommend that readers build fluency and reading speed before moving to higher levels.

How will this help my Chinese?

Reading extensively in a language you are learning is one of the most effective ways to build fluency. However, the key is to read at a high level of comprehension. Reading at the appropriate level in Chinese will increase your speed of character recognition, help you to acquire vocabulary faster, teach you to naturally learn grammar, and train your brain to think in Chinese. It also makes learning Chinese more fun and enjoyable. You will experience the sense of accomplishment and confidence that only comes from reading entire books in Chinese.

Extensive Reading

After years of studying Chinese, many people ask, "why can't I become fluent in Chinese?" Fluency can only happen when the language enters our "comfort zone." This comfort comes after significant exposure to and experience with the language. The more times you meet a word, phrase, or grammar point the more readily it will enter your comfort zone.

In the world of language research, experts agree that learners can acquire new vocabulary through reading only if the overall text can be understood. Decades of research indicate that if we know approximately 98% of the words in a book, we can comfortably "pick up" the 2% that is unfamiliar. Reading at this 98% comprehension level is referred to as "extensive reading."

Research in extensive reading has shown that it accelerates vocabulary learning and helps the learner to naturally understand grammar. Perhaps most importantly, it trains the brain to automatically recognize familiar language, thereby freeing up mental energy to focus on meaning and ideas. As they build reading speed and fluency, learners will move from reading "word by word" to processing "chunks of language." A defining feature is that it's less painful than the "intensive reading" commonly used in textbooks. In fact, extensive reading can be downright fun.

Graded Readers

Graded readers are the best books for learners to "extensively" read. Research has taught us that learners need to "encounter" a word 10-30 times before truly learning it, and often many more times for particularly complicated or abstract words. Graded readers are appropriate for learners because the language is controlled and simplified, as opposed to the language in native texts, which is inevitably difficult and often demotivating. Reading extensively with graded readers allows learners to bring together all of the language they have studied and absorb how the words naturally work together.

To become fluent, learners must not only understand the meaning of a word, but also understand its nuances, how to use it in conversation, how to pair it with other words, where it fits into natural word order, and how it is used in grammar structures. No textbook could ever be written to teach all of this explicitly. When used properly, a textbook introduces the language and provides the basic meanings, while graded readers consolidate, strengthen, and deepen understanding.

Without graded readers, learners would have to study dictionaries, textbooks, sample dialogs, and simple conversations until they have randomly encountered enough Chinese for it to enter their comfort zones. With proper use of graded readers, learners can tackle this issue and develop greater fluency now, at their current levels, instead of waiting until some period in the distant future. With a stronger foundation and greater confidence at their current levels, learners are encouraged and motivated to continue their Chinese studies to even greater heights. Plus, they'll quickly learn that reading Chinese is fun!

About Mandarin Companion

Mandarin Companion was started by Jared Turner and John Pasden who met one fateful day on a bus in Shanghai when the only remaining seat left them sitting next to each other. A year later, Jared had greatly improved his Chinese using extensive reading but was frustrated at the lack of suitable reading materials. He approached John with the prospect of creating their own series. Having worked in Chinese education for nearly a decade, John was intrigued with the idea and thus began the Mandarin Companion series.

John majored in Japanese in college, but started learning Mandarin and later moved to China where his learning accelerated. After developing language proficiency, he was admitted into an all-Chinese masters program in applied linguistics at East China Normal University in Shanghai. Throughout his learning process, John developed an open mind to different learning styles and a tendency to challenge conventional wisdom in the field of teaching Chinese. He has since worked at ChinesePod as academic director and host, and opened his own consultancy, AllSet Learning, in Shanghai to help individuals acquire Chinese language proficiency. He lives in Shanghai with his wife and children.

After graduate school and with no Chinese language skills, Jared decided to move to China with his young family in search of career opportunities. Later while working on an investment project, Jared learned about extensive reading and decided that if it was as effective as it claimed to be, it could help him learn Chinese. In three months, he read 10 Chinese graded readers and his language ability quickly improved from speaking words and phrases to a conversational level. Jared has an MBA from Purdue University and a bachelor in Economics from the University of Utah. He lives in Shanghai with his wife and children.

Credits

Original Author: Washington Irving

Editor-in-Chief: John Pasden

Adapted by: Yang Renjun

Content Editor: Yu Cui

Illustrator: Hu Shen

Producer: Jared Turner

Acknowledgments

We are grateful to Yang Renjun, Yu Cui, Song Shen and the entire team at AllSet Learning for working on this project and contributing the perfect mix of talent to produce this series.

Thank you to our enthusiastic testers, Ben Slye, Brandon Sanchez, Logan Pauley, and Ashlyn Weber.

A special thanks to Rob Waring, to whom we refer as the "godfather of extensive reading" for his encouragement, expert advice, and support with this project.

Thank you to Heather Turner for being the inspiration behind the entire series, and to Song Shen for supporting us, handling all the small thankless tasks, and spurring us forward if we dared to fall behind.

Moreover, we will be forever grateful for Yuehua Liu and Chengzhi Chu for pioneering the first graded readers in Chinese and to whom we owe a debt of gratitude for their years of tireless work to bring these type of materials to the Chinese learning community.

Table of Contents

Story Adaptation Notes

This story is an adaptation of American author Washington Irving's 1819 classic story, *Rip Van Winkle*. This Mandarin Companion graded reader has been adapted into a fully localized Chinese version of the original story. The characters have been given authentic Chinese names as opposed to transliterations of English names, which sound foreign in Chinese. The locations have been adapted to well-known places in China.

The story of Rip Van Winkle is an interesting case for adaptation because Chinese folklore has a similar story called 爛柯人 (Làn Kē Rén). In that story, the main character, 王質 (Wáng Zhì), was away for over 100 years in contrast to the American story where Rip Van Winkle slept for 20 years. This adaptation settled on the period of 60 years in order to span a specific time period in 20th century China for maximum dramatic effect.

Character Adaptations

The following is a list of the characters from *The Sixty Year Dream* in Chinese followed by their corresponding English names from Irving's original story. There are, of course, other characters in the story besides these, but many do not have exact correspondences to the original. The names below aren't translations; they're new Chinese names used for the Chinese versions of the original characters. Think of them as all-new characters in a Chinese story.

周學發 (Zhōu Xuéfā) - Rip Van Winkle

王小花 (Wáng Xiǎohuā) - Dame Van Winkle

小黑 (Xiǎo Hēi) - Wolf

周國平 (Zhōu Guópíng) - Rip Van Winkle, Jr.

周國英 (Zhōu Guóyīng) - Judith Gardenier

Cast of Characters

周學發
(Zhōu Xuéfā)

王小花
(Wáng Xiǎohuā)

小黑
(Xiǎo Hēi)

周國英
(Zhōu Guóyīng)

周歡歡
(Zhōu Huānhuān)

奇怪的老人
(Qíguài de Lǎorén)

劉老三
(Liú Lǎo Sān)

老張
(Lǎo Zhāng)

老胡
(Lǎo Hú)

Locations

北京 (Běijīng)

Beijing (formerly known as Peking), home of the last emperor of China and capital of modern-day China

香山 (Xiāng Shān)

Literally "Fragrant Mountains," a famous location to the west of Beijing

— **Chapter 1** —
1931 年

在北京，每個人都知道一個地方，叫
香山。香山 看到了北京 所有的 變化。它
看到過 住在北京 的第 一個皇帝，也看到過
最後 一個皇帝。它看到過 皇帝 的出生，也
看到過 皇帝 的死。香山 還看著每個北京
人的生活，它看著他們哭，也看著他們笑。
北京 人都覺得，香山 像一個不會說話的
老朋友。

　1931 年的北京 跟以前很不一樣 了。那
時候，中國已經沒有皇帝 了，人們都在想

1　變化 (biànhuà) *n.* change, changes
2　看到過 (kàndàoguò) *vc.* have seen (before)
3　第 (dì) *prefix* [ordinal marker for numbers, used in "first," "second," etc.]
4　皇帝 (huángdì) *n.* emperor
5　最後 (zuìhòu) *adj.* last, final
6　出生 (chūshēng) *n.* birth
7　生活 (shēnghuó) *n.* (daily) life
8　跟 ⋯⋯ 不一樣 (gēn⋯bù yīyàng) *phrase* not the same as…

中國以後會怎麼樣。人們真希望，香山可以告訴他們。

　　周學發 是一個北京 人，他的家在香山不遠的地方。周學發 的爸爸以前在有錢人家裡工作，每天總是 很早出門，很晚才回家。但是周學發 跟他爸爸很不一樣，他不關心 家裡的事，也不想工作，只喜歡玩，所以他一直 沒有錢。周學發 19 歲的時候，他爸爸媽媽幫 他找了個老婆，不久以後，他的爸爸媽媽就死了。

　　周學發 的老婆 叫王小花。王小花 是一個很有意思 的女人。她有點胖，說話

9　希望 (xīwàng) *v.* to hope
10　總是 (zǒngshì) *adv.* always
11　關心 (guānxīn) *v.* to be concerned about
12　一直 (yīzhí) *adv.* continuously, all along
13　幫 (bāng) *v.* to help

14　老婆 (lǎopo) *n.* wife (informal)
15　花 (huā) *v.* to spend
16　有意思 (yǒuyìsi) *adj.* interesting
17　胖 (pàng) *adj.* fat

很大聲。跟別的中國女人不同，她從來不

覺得女人應該聽男人的話。因為周學發 不

喜歡在家裡做事，也不想出去工作，所以

---

18 跟 ‧‧‧‧‧ 不同 (gēn…bùtóng)
phrase different from…

19 聽 ‧‧‧‧‧ 的話 (ting…dehuà)
phrase to listen to…, to do as… says

家裡的事總是 他老婆 做。這讓王小花 很生氣，她總是 對周學發 大聲說："我從來沒有見過像你這樣的男人。你為什麼從來不關心 家裡的事？如果我不跟你在一起，沒有女人會要你。"每次王小花 生氣 的時候，周學發 就像個孩子一樣，看著天，很長時間不說話。

周學發 和王小花 有一個兒子和一個女兒。兒子叫周國平，跟周學發 很像，每天都在外面 玩。他有很多朋友，他不喜歡跟周學發 一起玩。女兒叫周國英，比周國平 小，她不太喜歡出去玩，經常在家幫 王小花 做事。周學發 很喜歡他的女兒，在家的時候他經常跟女兒一起玩，給她做

很多好玩 的東西。可是如果王小花 看到
他跟女兒一起玩，就會很生氣，因為她覺
得周學發 應該多做一點家裡的事。

在家裡，周學發 只有一個朋友，就是
他的狗。這只狗 很黑，所以周學發 叫它
小黑。但是王小花 很不喜歡小黑，她生氣
的時候，也會大聲對小黑 說：“周學發 不
做事，都是你的錯。”所以小黑 很怕 王小
花，每次看到王小花，都會小心 地跑開。

---

22 好玩 (hǎowán) *adj.* fun
23 狗 (gǒu) *n.* dog
24 怕 (pà) *v.* to be afraid of

25 小心 (xiǎoxīn) *v.* to be careful
26 跑開 (pǎokāi) *vc.* to run away

Chapter 2
茶館裡的朋友

別人 都知道王小花 喜歡生氣，也都知道周學發 不喜歡在家裡做事，但是他們都很喜歡周學發。

周學發 是個奇怪 的人，他的想法跟別人很不一樣。他在家的時候，什麼事都不做，但是在外面，總是 喜歡幫 別人。他會幫 老人買東西，幫 女人打水、送水，給小孩子們做好玩 的東西。周學發 覺得，他幫 別人 的時候很開心。這就是奇怪 的周學發，他不喜歡做家裡的事，可是他

---

27 別人 (biérén) *n.* other people
28 奇怪 (qíguài) *adj.* strange
29 想法 (xiǎngfa) *n.* thinking, idea
30 打水 (dǎshuǐ) *vo.* to draw water (from a communal source)
31 送水 (sòngshuǐ) *vo.* to deliver water
32 開心 (kāixīn) *adj.* happy

喜歡幫 別人 做事。所有的人都很喜歡
周學發。因為周學發，別人 也很喜歡小黑。

但是因為這樣，王小花 總是 生氣。如
果別人 聽說王小花 又生氣 了，那他們一
定不會覺得這是周學發 的錯。王小花 生氣
的時候會說很多不好聽 的話。周學發 不
想聽，就和小黑 一起出門。

周學發 經常去一個茶館。在茶館 裡，
他有很多朋友。他們經常來茶館 裡喝茶，
一邊喝茶一邊談 國家大事。

劉老三 說："我覺得以前比現在好。以
前我爸爸為皇帝 工作，我們家很有錢，我
不用工作。現在如果我不工作，就沒有錢。
我希望 以後還會有皇帝。"

---

33 不好聽 (bùhǎotīng) *adj.*
bad-sounding, harsh, mean

34 茶館 (cháguǎn) *n.* tea house

35 談 (tán) *v.* to talk about, to discuss

　　老張 說："我覺得現在比以前好。以前

所有的錢都在皇帝 手裡，他高興的時候，
　　　　　　　　4

可以給我們很多東西。他不高興的時候，

可以讓我們死。"

周學發 說:"我覺得以前跟現在都一樣。
以前,我們要聽皇帝的話,可能 以後,我
們要聽下一個'皇帝'的話。所以,我們應該
讓自己開心,不要去想別的事。"

老胡 是這裡最老的人。只有他認識字,
別人 都不認識字。人們都知道他看過很
多書,所以很想聽他的想法。老胡 說:"你
們說的都不對。以後的中國跟以前不一樣,
跟現在也不一樣。中國不可能 再有皇帝。
以後的中國不是一個人的中國,是我們每
一個人的中國!"

周學發 覺得很奇怪:"中國不是一個
人的中國,是我們每一個人的中國。什
麼意思?"就在這個時候,王小花 跑進來,

---

36 跟……一樣 (gēn…yīyàng)   37 可能 (kěnéng) *adv.* possibly, maybe
phrase the same as…

看起來 很生氣，大聲對周學發 說："我知道
你又在這裡喝茶。家裡那麼多事，你不做，
你來這裡談 中國的事?"周學發 一下子 不
說話了，小黑 也小心 地走到別的地方。

然後，王小花 又生氣 地對周學發 的

38 看起來 (kànqǐlai) *v.* to appear, to
look (a certain way)

39 一下子 (yīxiàzi) *adv.* all at once, all
of a sudden

朋友說："他從來不關心 家裡的事，每天都
出來玩，跟你們一樣。他來茶館 喝茶、談
國家大事，一定是你們讓他來的。這都是
你們的錯！"周學發 的朋友們不知道應該
說什麼，因為他們從來沒有見過這樣的中
國女人，他們的老婆 都很聽話。周學發 覺
得這樣很沒面子，從那以後，他再也沒有
去過茶館。

---

40 聽話 (tīnghuà) *adj.* obedient
41 沒面子 (méimiànzi) *phrase*
   humiliating, lit. "to have no face"

42 再也沒有 (zài yě méiyǒu) *phrase*
   never again have

— Chapter 3 —
去香山

發生 這件事以後，周學發 很長時間都
不太開心。他沒有別的地方可以去，只能
帶小黑 去香山 走一走。

以前，周學發 經常和朋友去香山。他
們帶著刀，在香山 上用木頭 做很多好玩 的
東西。周國英 很喜歡她爸爸做的東西。她
最喜歡周學發 做的四個小木頭人。周國英
覺得這四個小木頭人 應該是一家人，他們
是爸爸、媽媽、哥哥和妹妹，他們一直 在
一起，一直 很開心。每次周學發 看到女兒
跟這四個小木頭人 一起玩，他都覺得有點

---

43 發生 (fāshēng) v. to happen, to
occur

44 木頭 (mùtou) n. wood

45 小木頭人 (xiǎo mùtou rén) *phrase*
little wooden figurine

難過。

現在，周學發 和小黑 坐在地上，很長時間只看著天，不說話。過了一會兒，周學發 對小黑 說："小黑，我現在只有你一個朋友了，只有你還關心 我。我知道你也很難過，但是你放心，我會一直 和你在一起。"小黑 看了一下周學發，好像 在說："我知道！放心 吧，我也會一直 和你在一起。"

周學發 看了一下他手裡的刀，又想到了一個女孩。這個女孩是他以前的女朋友，跟他是同一個姓，叫周歡歡，長得 很可愛。周學發 一直 很喜歡她，她也喜歡周學發。天氣好的時候，他們經常一起去

---

46 難過 (nánguò) *adj.* sad, upset
47 地上 (dìshang) *n.* on the ground
48 放心 (fàngxīn) *v.* to rest assured, to not worry
49 好像 (hǎoxiàng) *v.* it seems that

50 長得 (zhǎngde) *v.* to (physically) look (a certain way)

香山 玩。每次去香山，周學發 都帶著刀，給周歡歡 做很多好看 的東西。他們在一起很開心。他們 18 歲的時候，周學發 做了一個很漂亮 的木頭 房子，送給了周歡歡。現在周學發 還記得，他送給周歡歡 這個木頭 房子的時候，說："這是我們以後的家。希望 我們一直 在一起，一直 很開心。"周歡歡 笑了，她真的很開心！

可是，周學發 和周歡歡 的家人都不希望 他們在一起。一個原因 是周歡歡 的爸爸媽媽聽說周學發 不喜歡工作，一直 都花 他爸爸的錢。如果他爸爸死了，他怎麼辦？還有一個原因，就是他們都姓周。在那個時候，住在同一個地方的人，如果是

---

51 好看 (hǎokàn) *adj.* good-looking
52 漂亮 (piàoliang) *adj.* pretty
53 記得 (jìde) *v.* to remember
54 原因 (yuányīn) *n.* cause, reason

同一個姓，他們會覺得是同一家人，所以

不能在一起。

　　後來，周歡歡 的爸爸給她找了一個老

公，她去了很遠的地方。因為周學發 只喜

歡玩，周學發 的爸爸幫 他找了一個老婆，
就是王小花。小花 不太好看，但是很會做
事。

　　周學發 和周歡歡 很多年沒有見面了，
周學發 看著天，心裡想："歡歡，你現在怎
麼樣了？你會想我嗎？"

　　這個時候天快黑了。他不想回家，可
是沒有辦法，他怕 王小花，如果天黑以後
他不回家，王小花 就會對他生氣 地大叫。
他不開心 地對小黑 說："我們快回家吧。
要不然 她又要對我們大叫了。"可是就在
他要下山 的時候，周學發 好像 聽到有人
在叫他的名字，但是聲音 很遠："周學發！
周學發……"

---

56 要不然 (yàoburán) *conj.* otherwise
57 下山 (xiàshān) *vo.* to go down the
mountain

58 聲音 (shēngyīn) *n.* sound, voice

Chapter 4
奇怪的老人

聽到有人叫他的名字的時候，周學發往左右看了一下，沒有看到山上有人。他想："這不是真的，一定是我聽錯了。"可是不知道為什麼，這個聲音 讓小黑 覺得可怕，馬上 跑到了周學發 的身後。

但是，過了一會兒，周學發 又聽到那個聲音："周學發！周學發……"聲音 比剛才 近了很多，好像 在他的後面。小黑好像 更怕 了。周學發 也有點兒怕 了，他想："平時 這裡沒有人。這麼晚了，誰會上山？"

---

59 可怕 (kěpà) *adj.* frightening, scary
60 馬上 (mǎshàng) *adv.* right away
61 剛才 (gāngcái) *tn.* just now

62 平時 (píngshí) *adv.* usually, normally
63 上山 (shàngshān) *vo.* to go up the mountain

周學發 又往後面看。他看到一個奇怪的老人。那個老人看起來 很瘦，頭髮 很長，但是都白了，還拿了一個大包，包裡好像 有很多東西。最奇怪 的是，那個老人穿著幾百年以前的衣服。

老人看到 周學發 以後，笑著對他說：「你能幫 我嗎？我的東西太多了，我拿不動，希望 你可以幫 我。」

周學發 說：「沒問題。你的家在哪兒？遠嗎？」

老人又笑了一下，說：「不太遠，就在香山 的北邊。」

周學發 覺得更奇怪 了，他以前經常來香山，但是他知道平時 沒有人住在北

---

64 瘦 (shòu) *adj*. thin
65 頭髮 (tóufà) *n*. hair

66 拿不動 (nábudòng) *vc*. cannot move, cannot carry

邊。他有點怕，但是看到老人太老了，他
覺得應該幫 一下老人。小黑 很怕 這個老
人，但是沒有辦法，它只能跟周學發 一起
去老人的家。

在路上，周學發 和老人都沒有說話。

周學發 想："為什麼這個老人知道我的名字？為什麼他看起來 這麼奇怪？為什麼他一個人在這裡？為什麼他住在這個沒有人的山上？我應該問問他。"但是周學發 還是有點怕 這個老人，所以一直 沒有問。

走了很長時間，天已經很黑了，他們才到了老人的家。老人的家很奇怪，外面看起來 不像一個房子，像一個山洞，一點都不像人住的地方。但是他們一起進了山洞 以後，周學發 才發現 自己到了一個很不一樣的地方。他沒說話，但是心裡在大聲說："天啊！這是哪裡？我到了天上嗎？"

---

67 山洞 (shāndòng) *n.* cave
68 發現 (fāxiàn) *v.* to discover
69 天上 (tiānshàng) *n.* in heaven

Chapter 5
老人不見了！

周學發 從來沒有見過這麼漂亮 的地方。這個地方天氣很好，他看到很多樹，樹上都是好吃的水果。不遠的地方還有小河，河裡有很多好看 的小魚，河邊都是漂亮 的花。

"太美了！這麼漂亮 的地方，我以前怎麼從來沒有發現？"周學發 想。但是看到老人的樣子 和衣服，他又覺得奇怪："不對，這裡一定不是人住的地方。我真的到了天上 嗎？"想到這裡，他覺得很開心，但又覺得有點怕。小黑 一直 小心 地走在

70 小河 (xiǎohé) *n.* stream, lit. "small river"　71 樣子 (yàngzi) *n.* appearance

周學發 的後面，一點聲音 都沒有，它覺得
他們真不應該來這裡。

後來，老人帶他來到一個很漂亮 的
木頭 房子，請周學發 坐下。這個時候，老
人才說話。他還是笑著說："你真是個好
人！在香山 上，我看到了好幾個人，但是
只有你幫 了我的忙。我一定要謝謝你！"
周學發 聽了，馬上 說："這是我應該做的。
你不用謝我！我一會兒要下山。"老人又對
房子外面 大聲說："快拿酒和菜進來！"然
後，周學發 看到幾個漂亮 的女人拿了很
多酒和菜進來，然後就出去了。她們的衣
服和老人一樣，都是幾百年以前的。

老人說："這是好酒，你一定從來沒有
喝過。喝點吧！"周學發 喝了以後，馬上

說:"好酒！真是好酒！我真的從來沒有喝過這麼好的酒！"可是他還是覺得所有的事都太奇怪了，他應該問問老人。他說:"你能告訴我這是哪裡嗎？你說這是你的家，可是我沒看到你的家人。你穿著很多年以前的衣服，我覺得很奇怪。"老人又笑了，說:"你放心，我不是壞人。你先別問這麼多，先喝酒，喝了酒以後你就知道了。"

喝酒的時候，老人問周學發:"你為什麼一個人在山上？"周學發覺得很不好意思，因為如果告訴老人他怕老婆，會很沒面子。所以他很長時間都沒有說話。老人笑了笑，然後又問他:"你覺得現在好嗎？"周學發笑了一下，說:"現在？現在很

---

72 不好意思 (bùhǎoyìsi) *adj.*
embarrassed

好，中國已經沒有皇帝 了。如果家裡也沒
有'皇帝'，就更好了！"老人又笑了，說："你
家裡的'皇帝'是你老婆 嗎？"周學發 什麼都
沒說。後來 他跟老人喝了很多酒，很快就

睡著 了。
73

　周學發 睡了很長時間，可是他睡醒 的
74
時候，發現 自己不在老人的山洞 裡，他又
68   67
回到了看到老人的地方。

73 睡著 (shuìzháo) *vc.* to fall asleep　74 睡醒 (shuìxǐng) *vc.* to awake from sleep

所有的事周學發 都記得：看到老人，幫 老人拿東西，去老人的家，喝老人的酒……"可是我現在怎麼在這裡？我不是應該在老人的家裡嗎？"周學發 覺得很奇怪。他又發現 小黑 不見了，他馬上 大聲叫："小黑！小黑 ……"可是，最後 小黑都沒有出現。"那個老人讓我喝那麼多酒，一定是想等我睡著 了，然後帶走小黑。太過分 了！我要去找小黑。"

---

75 出現 (chūxiàn) *v.* to appear   76 過分 (guòfèn) *adj.* going too far

Chapter 6
這是北京嗎？

周學發 想從地上 起來的時候，他覺得自己的身體跟以前有點不同，但是不知道哪裡不同。後來 他到了一個小河 邊，從河裡他看到了自己。他覺得自己看起來 像一個八九十歲 的老人，頭髮 和胡子 又白又長，衣服也很破 了。還有，他上山 的時候帶的刀也壞了。

"天啊！我怎麼了？誰能告訴我？"他大聲說。

他覺得自己現在的身體很不好，不能走得很快。花 了很長時間，周學發 才

---

77 八九十歲 (bā-jiǔshí suì) *phrase* 80 or 90 years old

78 鬍子 (húzi) *n.* beard

79 破 (pò) *adj.* worn out

來到香山 的北邊。可是他沒有找到老人
的家。"太奇怪 了！我記得 他家就在這個
山洞 裡，可是為什麼不見了？"周學發 對自
己說。然後，他在那裡大聲叫"小黑！小黑
……"可是小黑 還是沒有出現。周學發 很
難過。

沒有別的辦法，他只能下山 回家。在
路上，周學發 很不開心。他不知道自己為
什麼會變成 這樣，不知道以後能不能再看
到小黑，也不知道回家以後，老婆 會怎麼
樣。"她一定很生氣！我從來沒有在外面 這
麼長時間。她看到我這個樣子 會怎麼樣？
我應該怎麼對她說這些事？"周學發 想。

可是，他覺得有點兒奇怪："平時 香山
上的人一直 不多，可是今天怎麼這麼多
人上山？還有，為什麼我都不認識他們？"
更讓他覺得奇怪 的是，這些人的衣服
跟他的也很不同。女人的衣服很短，這讓
周學發 很不好意思。

走了一會兒，他又看到一些漂亮 的房

---

80 變成 (biànchéng) *vc.* to turn into　　81 短 (duǎn) *adj.* short

子。"不對啊，這裡沒有房子，怎麼一下子

出現 這麼多房子？我在做夢 嗎？"周學發
　　39　　　　　　　　　　　　　82

覺得越來越 奇怪 了。"一定是那些酒有問
　　　83　　28

---

82 做夢 (zuòmèng) *vo.* to dream

83 越來越 (yuèláiyuè) *adv.* more and
more

題，要不然 我怎麼會看到這麼多奇怪 的
東西。"周學發 對自己說。

周學發 快到家的時候，他看到很多
人，可是這些人他都不認識。他們穿著很
奇怪 的衣服，也一直 看著周學發。這讓
周學發 一下子 不知道怎麼辦。

周學發 發現，北京 好像 發生 了很大
的變化，他走了很長時間都沒找到自己的
家。"我真的在做夢 嗎？這裡以前都是樹和
花，怎麼現在都是房子？這些房子怎麼那
麼高？希望 這都不是真的。"周學發 在心
裡問自己，"一定是昨天的酒有問題！我要
快點回家睡覺，可能 睡醒 以後就會好的。"

— Chapter 7 —
什麼？我死了？

走了很久，周學發 才找到自己的家。他一直 在想王小花 會怎麼對他。

可是，到了門外的時候，周學發 發現，自己的家跟昨天很不一樣，現在房子看起來很老。更奇怪 的是，他一點也不認識開門的人。

"你是誰？你怎麼在我家裡？"周學發 有點生氣，問他。

"這是我家，你是誰？"那個人也有點生氣。他看著周學發，覺得周學發 有點可怕。他從來沒有看到過 這樣的老人，胡子 那麼長，頭發 也那麼長，衣服是破

的。"你快走，走！"那個人又說。

　　周學發 更生氣 了，"你太過分 了！這
是我家，為什麼要我走？你出去！"周學發
大聲說。聽到他們這麼說，很多人都走過

來看。

一個女人問周學發：“你是誰？你怎麼看起來 這麼奇怪？我們都知道他住在這裡十幾年了，這裡怎麼可能 是你家？”然後，女人又小聲跟開門的人說：“這個人一定有問題，你進去吧，別再給他開門了。”

“小花，小花……”周學發 大聲叫他的老婆，但是王小花 沒有出現。“你們看到我老婆 王小花 了嗎？”周學發 問。那個女人說：“這裡沒有人叫王小花，你一定走錯地方了。”

周學發 很生氣，他覺得這些人很過分。但是他不知道應該怎麼辦。沒有別的辦法，他只能去茶館 找他的朋友，讓他們來告訴這些人，這裡就是他的家。

周學發 走在去茶館 的路上，發現 路比
以前好了很多，人也比以前多了很多。更
奇怪 的是，他看到了很多車。"怎麼一下子
有這麼多車？為什麼每個人都會開車？"
周學發 不明白為什麼一天的時間會發生
這麼多變化。

周學發 來到茶館，他發現 這裡跟昨
天也有一些不同。"怎麼變這麼漂亮 了？這
裡怎麼有這麼多人？他們好像 都在談 自
己的事。"就在周學發 要進去的時候，一個
男人走過來，大聲對他說："出去，出去，
要飯的 不能進去。"

周學發 聽他這樣說，覺得很沒面子。
他很生氣，大聲說："我不是要飯的，我是

來找我朋友的。"

"你來這裡找朋友？誰是你的朋友？你

看看你，胡子 和頭髮 這麼長，衣服也破
　　　　　　78　　65　　　　　　　79

了。來我們這裡喝茶的人都是有錢人，誰會關心一個要飯的？你快出去。"那個男人說。

周學發 想："我今天一定要找到一個朋友，要不然 我就不能回家了。"然後他就走進茶館 大聲叫："劉老三，老張，老胡，你們在哪裡？"可是他的朋友都沒有出現。最後，一個老人走過來，看了看周學發，說："我認識劉老三，你是誰？"周學發 很高興有人認識他的朋友，馬上 說："我叫周學發，是他的朋友。你知道他在哪裡嗎？"

那個老人聽到 周學發 的話，馬上說："什麼？你是周學發？怎麼可能！你不是死了嗎？"

"什麼？我死了？"聽他這樣說，周學發

覺得很可怕！

— Chapter 8 —
1991 年

老人很快去找到了周學發的女兒。周學發看到女兒的時候，不知道應該說什麼，因為她已經是一個六七十歲的老人了。

周學發的女兒也覺得很奇怪。周學發已經六十年沒有出現了，她已經不太記得爸爸的樣子了，所以她也不知道這個人是不是她爸爸。她問周學發："你真的是我爸爸？我怎麼知道這是不是真的？"周學發看著女兒，他也覺得所有的事都太奇怪了，他也想快點知道發生了什麼事。

"你媽媽是不是叫王小花？你哥哥是不是叫周國平？你家是不是有一隻狗叫

小黑？你還記得 我給你做的小木頭人 嗎？
你還記得 你小時候，我經常帶你去河邊玩
嗎？"

"爸爸，你真的是我爸爸。我不是在
做夢。這六十年你都去了哪裡？為什麼不
回家？"

"什麼？六十年？我昨天去香山，今天回來。怎麼是六十年？"周學發 馬上 問。

"現在是 1991 年了！"周國英 也覺得很奇怪，她想："是不是爸爸老了，以前的事都忘了？"

"我只是在香山 上睡了一覺，怎麼一下子 到了 1991 年？ 小黑 跟我一起去香山 的，小黑 在哪兒？"周學發 很 關心小黑。

"你上山 的那天晚上，小黑 就回來了。可是你沒有跟他一起回來，小黑 一直 在等你，它等了你很多年，最後 就死了。爸爸，你在說什麼？"周國英 一點都不明白周學發 的話。

"啊！那個老人太過分 了。一定是因

為那個酒，一定是！"看看自己又長又白的頭髮 和鬍子，周學發 說，"昨天，不，六十年前，我和小黑 去了香山。快下山 的時候，我看到一個老人，他穿著幾百年以前的衣服，讓我幫 他拿東西。我記得 他請我喝了很多好酒，然後我就睡著 了。等我睡醒 的時候，已經是今天早上了。然後我下山 回家，看到我們的家變了，茶館 變了，你也變了。"周學發 說得很快，他很想告訴別人 這件事，可是好像 沒有人覺得他說的是真的。

　　"天啊！誰能告訴我發生 了什麼！我們都以為你已經死了！"周國英 說。

— Chapter 9 —
六十年的事

最後，周學發 去了女兒的家。周國英
現在有三個孩子，都不跟她住在一起，現
在家裡只有她和她老公兩個人。

對周學發 來說，現在所有的東西都是
新的。現在，周學發 就像一個孩子，又
好奇 又小心 地看著女兒的家，看著現在所
有的變化。他從來沒有住過這麼高的房子。
房子裡的很多東西，他從來都沒有看到過。
但是在女兒的家裡，也有他認識的東西，
就是那四個小木頭人！周學發 看著這四個
小木頭人，兩個大的，兩個小的，很開心

86 好奇 (hàoqí) *adj.* curious

地坐在一起。他一下子 很難過，哭了。

周國英 讓周學發 穿上她老公的衣服，

說：“爸爸，你坐在這裡吧。我很好奇，我

有很多事要告訴你。"

"我怎麼沒有看到你媽媽和你哥哥?"周學發 問。

"這六十年,發生 了很多很多事。你走了以後,我們的生活 越來越 難。1937 年的時候,中國和日本發生 了戰爭。哥哥去了以後就一直 沒有回來。後來 聽說他在戰爭 中死了。"說到這裡,周國英 一下子哭了。

"啊!那你媽媽呢?"周學發 也哭了。

"哥哥死了以後,媽媽天天難過,身體越來越 不好,越來越 瘦。1961 年的時候,很多人都沒有東西吃。媽媽為了我,自己吃得很少。後來,她也去世了。"周國英

87 戰爭 (zhànzhēng) *n.* war

難過 地說。
₄₆

　　"他們都死了！他們都死了……我還活著！"周學發 越來越 難過，他真希望 這不是真的。"那現在中國的 皇帝 是誰？"周學發 又問。

　　"中國再也沒有 皇帝 了！中國再也不是一個人的中國，是我們每一個人的中國。"周國英 說。

　　"中國是我們每一個人的中國……"周學發 記得 以前好像 有人這樣說過。

　　"爸爸，以前的那個房子，現在已經不是我們的了。以後你就跟我們一起住吧。你真的只在香山 上睡了一晚？可是我們這裡已經過了六十年！"周國英 還是覺

---

88 活著 (huózhe) vc. living　　　　89 再也不 (zài yě bù) phrase never again

得太奇怪了！不只是她，所有的人都覺得
奇怪。

"我也想知道為什麼會這樣。我只睡了
一晚，我的六十年一下子就沒有了。我老
了這麼多，你也一下子從小孩變成了老
人。這裡的房子、衣服、路都變了，還有

很多新東西我都不認識。一點都不好玩。
誰能告訴我，我是死了還是活著？我是醒
了還是在做夢？"說完，周學發 像小孩子一
樣又哭了。

Chapter 10
六十年的夢

後來，周學發 一直 和女兒一起生活。
他還是像六十年前一樣，什麼事都不做，
每天都出去走走。

他經常去以前住的地方，他發現 那裡
比以前方便 多了。人們不用每天出門去
打水，因為每家都有自來水。人們出門也
比以前方便 多了，因為很多人都有車。但
是，他發現，人們都太忙了，人們的想法
也跟以前不一樣 了。沒有人想花 時間去幫
別人，也沒有人會在路上對他笑。小孩子
看起來 也不太開心，因為他們總是 有很多

---

90 方便 (fāngbiàn) *adj.* convenient　　91 自來水 (zìláishuǐ) *n.* tap water

東西要學。更讓他難過 的是，小河 一點都
不好玩 了，河裡沒有魚了，因為河裡的水
沒有以前好了。樹和花 都少了很多，因為
以前有樹和花 的地方都有了很高的房子。

周學發 還是經常去那個茶館。他以前的朋友，有的死了，有的還活著。但是現在，周學發 更喜歡和年輕人在一起。那些年輕人很喜歡聽他說六十年前的事。

過了很長時間，周學發 才明白這六十年發生 了什麼。他知道中國發生 過很大的戰爭。因為那次戰爭，中國跟以前不一樣了。只是有時候，他還是像以前一樣，看著天，很長時間都不說話。沒有人知道他是喜歡現在的生活，還是希望 回到以前。

人們知道周學發 的事以後，都很關心他。很多年輕人都很好奇 那個奇怪 的老人和他的山洞 在哪裡，他們也想喝一點老人的酒。周學發 問他們："你為什麼想喝老人的酒？"

有的人說:"我希望 我醒了的時候發現自己有很多錢。"

有的人說:"我希望 醒了的時候發現自己在一個更有意思 的地方。"

有的人說:"我希望 看看六十年後中國會變成 什麼樣子。"

周學發 慢慢明白了北京 和北京 人的變化,但是他還是不知道現在的北京 是不是一個夢。天氣好的時候,他還是會上山走走。但是他再也沒有 看到過 那個奇怪的老人和他的木頭 房子。有一次,周學發又在香山 上睡著 了,在夢裡,他好像 又回到了 1931 年。

Key Words 關鍵詞 (Guānjiàncí)

1. 變化 (biànhuà) *n.* change, changes
2. 看到過 (kàndàoguò) *vc.* have seen (before)
3. 第 (dì) *prefix* [ordinal marker for numbers, used in "first," "second," etc.]
4. 皇帝 (huángdì) *n.* emperor
5. 最後 (zuìhòu) *adj.* last, final
6. 出生 (chūshēng) *n.* birth
7. 生活 (shēnghuó) *n.* (daily) life
8. 跟……不一樣 (gēn…bù yīyàng) *phrase* not the same as…
9. 希望 (xīwàng) *v.* to hope
10. 總是 (zǒngshì) *adv.* always
11. 關心 (guānxīn) *v.* to be concerned about
12. 一直 (yīzhí) *adv.* continuously, all along
13. 幫 (bāng) *v.* to help
14. 老婆 (lǎopo) *n.* wife (informal)
15. 花 (huā) *v.* to spend
16. 有意思 (yǒuyìsi) *adj.* interesting
17. 胖 (pàng) *adj.* fat
18. 跟……不同 (gēn…bùtóng) *phrase* different from…
19. 聽……的話 (ting…dehuà) *phrase* to listen to…, to do as… says
20. 生氣 (shēngqì) *v.* to get angry
21. 外面 (wàimiàn) *n.* outside
22. 好玩 (hǎowán) *adj.* fun
23. 狗 (gǒu) *n.* dog
24. 怕 (pà) *v.* to be afraid of
25. 小心 (xiǎoxīn) *v.* to be careful
26. 跑開 (pǎokāi) *vc.* to run away
27. 別人 (biérén) *n.* other people
28. 奇怪 (qíguài) *adj.* strange
29. 想法 (xiǎngfa) *n.* thinking, idea

30. 打水 (dǎshuǐ) *vo.* to draw water (from a communal source)

31. 送水 (sòngshuǐ) *vo.* to deliver water

32. 開心 (kāixīn) *adj.* happy

33. 不好聽 (bùhǎotīng) *adj.* bad-sounding, harsh, mean

34. 茶館 (cháguǎn) *n.* tea house

35. 談 (tán) *v.* to talk about, to discuss

36. 跟⋯⋯一樣 (gēn⋯yīyàng) *phrase* the same as...

37. 可能 (kěnéng) *adv.* possibly, maybe

38. 看起來 (kànqǐlai) *v.* to appear, to look (a certain way)

39. 一下子 (yīxiàzi) *adv.* all at once, all of a sudden

40. 聽話 (tīnghuà) *adj.* obedient

41. 沒面子 (méimiànzi) *phrase* humiliating, lit. "to have no face"

42. 再也沒有 (zài yě méiyǒu) *phrase* never again have

43. 發生 (fāshēng) *v.* to happen, to occur

44. 木頭 (mùtou) *n.* wood

45. 小木頭人 (xiǎo mùtou rén) *phrase* little wooden figurine

46. 難過 (nánguò) *adj.* sad, upset

47. 地上 (dìshang) *n.* on the ground

48. 放心 (fàngxīn) *v.* to rest assured, to not worry

49. 好像 (hǎoxiàng) *v.* it seems that

50. 長得 (zhǎngde) *v.* to (physically) look (a certain way)

51. 好看 (hǎokàn) *adj.* good-looking

52. 漂亮 (piàoliang) *adj.* pretty

53. 記得 (jìde) *v.* to remember

54. 原因 (yuányīn) *n.* cause, reason

55. 後來 (hòulái) *tn.* afterwards

56. 要不然 (yàoburán) *conj.* otherwise

57. 下山 (xiàshān) *vo.* to go down the mountain

58. 聲音 (shēngyīn) *n.* sound, voice

59. 可怕 (kěpà) *adj.* frightening, scary

60. 馬上 (mǎshàng) *adv.* right away

61. 剛才 (gāngcái) *tn.* just now

62. 平時 (píngshí) *adv.* usually, normally

63. 上山 (shàngshān) *vo.* to go up the mountain

64. 瘦 (shòu) *adj.* thin

65. 頭髮 (tóufà) *n.* hair

66. 拿不動 (nábudòng) *vc.* cannot move, cannot carry

67. 山洞 (shāndòng) *n.* cave

68. 發現 (fāxiàn) *v.* to discover

69. 天上 (tiānshàng) *n.* in heaven

70. 小河 (xiǎohé) *n.* stream, lit. "small river"

71. 樣子 (yàngzi) *n.* appearance

72. 不好意思 (bùhǎoyìsi) *adj.* embarrassed

73. 睡著 (shuìzháo) *vc.* to fall asleep

74. 睡醒 (shuìxǐng) *vc.* to awake from sleep

75. 出現 (chūxiàn) *v.* to appear

76. 過分 (guòfèn) *adj.* going too far

77. 八九十歲 (bā-jiǔshí suì) *phrase* 80 or 90 years old

78. 鬍子 (húzi) *n.* beard

79. 破 (pò) *adj.* worn out

80. 變成 (biànchéng) *vc.* to turn into

81. 短 (duǎn) *adj.* short

82. 做夢 (zuòmèng) *vo.* to dream

83. 越來越 (yuèláiyuè) *adv.* more and more

84. 睡覺 (shuìjiào) *vo.* to sleep

85. 要飯的 (yàofànde) *n.* a beggar

86. 好奇 (hàoqí) *adj.* curious

87. 戰爭 (zhànzhēng) *n.* war

88. 活著 (huózhe) *vc.* living

89. 再也不 (zài yě bù) *phrase* never again

90. 方便 (fāngbiàn) *adj.* convenient

91. 自來水 (zìláishuǐ) *n.* tap water

Part of Speech Key

adj. Adjective

adv. Adverb

aux. Auxiliary Verb

conj. Conjunction

cov. Coverb

mw. Measure word

n. Noun

on. Onomatopoeia

part. Particle

prep. Preposition

pn. Proper noun

tn. Time Noun

v. Verb

vc. Verb plus complement

vo. Verb plus object

Discussion Questions
討論問題 (Tǎolùn Wèntí)

Chapter 1 1931 年

1. 請你介紹一下周學發和他的家人。

2. 周學發的父母幫他找了一個老婆，你覺得他們做得對嗎？為什麼？

3. 你覺得中國女人都像王小花一樣嗎？為什麼？

4. 王小花從來不覺得女人應該聽男人的話，你覺得她的想法對嗎？

Chapter 2 茶館裡的朋友

1. 周學發和他的朋友在茶館裡討論什麼？他們的想法是什麼？

2. 像周學發這樣的老公，你覺得怎麼樣？

3. 中國人覺得，女人在外面，應該給老公面子。你怎麼看？

4. 你有沒有遇到過讓你很沒面子的事？請說一下。

Chapter 3 去香山

1. 周學發和周歡歡想在一起，可是他們的父母不讓他們在一起。你覺得對嗎？為什麼？

2. 以前在中國，住在同一個地方的男人和女人，如果是同一個姓，就不可以在一起。這是為什麼？這樣的事在你的國家發生過嗎？

3. 如果你的家人、朋友讓你很沒面子，你會怎麼做？

Chapter 4 奇怪的老人

1. 你覺得那個奇怪的老人是什麼人？

2. 你去過哪些山？你覺得它們怎麼樣？

Chapter 5 老人不見了!

1. 你覺得你去過的最漂亮的地方是哪裡？為什麼？

2. 你第一次喝酒是什麼時候？請說一個跟喝酒有關的有意思的事。

3. 現在在中國，很多人家裡都只有一個孩子，這個孩子就是家裡的"小皇帝"。你聽說過"小皇帝"嗎？你對"小皇帝"怎麼看？

Chapter 6 這是北京嗎？

1. 周學發睡醒以後發生了什麼？

2. 如果你是周學發，你發現自己一下子變老了，會怎麼辦？

3. 如果一個東西可以讓你變老或者變小，你想要嗎？為什麼？

Chapter 7 什麼？我死了？

1. 周學發在他的家和以前的茶館裡，遇到了什麼人？發生了什麼事？

2. 如果有人向你要飯、要錢，你會怎麼做？為什麼？

3. 如果你一個晚上沒有回家，你回家的時候發現自己變老了，你的父母不認識你了。怎麼辦？

Chapter 8 1991 年

1. 你知道六十年裡，中國發生了什麼變化嗎？

2. 1991 年的時候，你在哪裡？從那個時候到現在，你的國家發生了什麼變化？

3. 你覺得是什麼讓周學發一下子老了六十歲？

Chapter 9 六十年的事

1. 周國英告訴周學發，在六十年裡，他的家發生了什麼變化？

2. 你的國家以前有過戰爭嗎？請說一說你對戰爭的看法。

Chapter 10 六十年的夢

1. 你覺得周學發更喜歡 1931 年還是 1991 年？為什麼？

2. 如果你可以喝老人的酒，你希望發生什麼變化？

3. 你希望自己老了以後的生活是什麼樣的？

4. 如果你寫這個故事，你會怎麼寫？

Appendix A:
Character Comparison Reference

This appendix is designed to help Chinese teachers and learners use the Mandarin Companion graded readers as a companion to the most popular university textbooks and the HSK word lists.

The tables below compare the characters and vocabulary used in other study materials with those found in this Mandarin Companion graded reader. The tables below will display the exact characters and vocabulary used in this book and not covered by these sources. A learner who has studied these textbooks will likely find it easier to read this graded reader by focusing on these characters and words.

Integrated Chinese Level 1, Part 1-2 (3rd Ed.)

Words and characters in this story not covered by these textbooks:

Character	Pinyin	Word(s)	Pinyin
山	shān	香山 山上 上山 山洞 下山	Xiāng Shān shān shàng shàngshān shāndòng xiàshān
奇	qí	奇怪 好奇	qíguài hàoqí
怪	guài	奇怪	qíguài
聲	shēng	大聲 聲音	dàshēng shēngyīn
酒	jiǔ	好酒	hǎo jiǔ
帝	dì	皇帝	huángdì
皇	huáng	皇帝	huángdì
變	biàn	變化 變成	biànhuà biànchéng
木	mù	木頭 木頭人	mùtou mùtourén

Character	Pinyin	Word(s)	Pinyin
婆	pó	老婆	lǎopo
河	hé	河邊	hébiān
門	mén	出門	chūmén
		門外	mén wài
		開門	kāi mén
胡	hú	老胡	Lǎo Hú
		鬍子	húzi
總	zǒng	總是	zǒngshì
醒	xǐng	睡醒	shuì xǐng
夢	mèng	做夢	zuòmèng
洞	shù	樹	shù
周	dòng	山洞	shāndòng
戰	zhàn	戰爭	zhànzhēng
刀	dāo	刀	dāo
爭	zhēng	戰爭	zhànzhēng
輕	qīng	年輕人	niánqīngrén
破	pò	破	pò
劉	Liú	劉老三	Liú Lǎosān
原	yuán	原因	yuányīn
世	shì	去世	qùshì

New Practical Chinese Reader, Books 1-2 (1st Ed.)

Words and characters in this story not covered by these textbooks:

Character	Pinyin	Word(s)	Pinyin
周	zhōu	周學發	Zhōu Xuéfā
		周國平	Zhōu Guópíng
		周國英	Zhōu Guóyīng
奇	qí	奇怪	qíguài
		好奇	hàoqí

Character	Pinyin	Word(s)	Pinyin
怪	guài	奇怪	qíguài
直	zhí	一直	yīzhí
帝	dì	皇帝	huángdì
皇	huáng	皇帝	huángdì
木	mù	木頭 木頭人	mùtou mùtourén
希	xī	希望	xīwàng
望	wàng	希望	xīwàng
更	gèng	更	gèng
河	hé	河邊	hébiān
胡	hú	老胡 鬍子	Lǎo Hú húzi
醒	xǐng	睡醒	shuì xǐng
洞	dòng	做夢	zuòmèng
談	tán	樹	shù
戰	zhàn	山洞	shāndòng
爭	zhēng	戰爭	zhànzhēng
破	pò	刀	dāo
劉	liú	戰爭	zhànzhēng
原	yuán	年輕人	niánqīngrén
魚	yú	破	pò
近	jìn	劉老三	Liú Lǎosān
胖	pàng	原因	yuányīn
世	shì	去世	qùshì

Hanyu Shuiping Kaoshi (HSK) Levels 1-3

Words and characters in this story not covered by these levels:

Character	Pinyin	Word(s)	Pinyin
知	zhī	知道	zhīdao
王	wáng	王小花	Wáng Xiǎohuā
像	xiàng	好像 不像	hǎoxiàng bù xiàng
從	cóng	從來	cónglái
帝	dì	皇帝	huángdì
皇	huáng	皇帝	huángdì
死	sǐ	死	sǐ
英	yīng	周國英	Zhōu Guóyīng
木	mù	木頭 木頭人	mùtou mùtourén
更	gèng	更	gèng
婆	pó	老婆	lǎopo
活	huó	生活 活著	shēnghuó huózhe
胡	hú	老胡 鬍子	Lǎo Hú húzi
夢	mèng	做夢	zuòmèng
醒	xǐng	睡醒	shuì xǐng
洞	dòng	山洞	shāndòng
洞	tán	談	tán
刀	dāo	刀	dāo
戰	zhàn	戰爭	zhànzhēng
爭	zhēng	戰爭	zhànzhēng
劉	Liú	劉老三	Liú Lǎosān
破	pò	破	pò
往	wǎng	往	wǎng

Character	Pinyin	Word(s)	Pinyin
原	yuán	原因	yuányīn
美	měi	美	měi

Appendix B: Grammar Point Index

For learners new to reading Chinese, an understanding of grammar points can be extremely helpful for learners and teachers. The following is a list of the most challenging grammar points used in this graded reader.

These grammar points correspond to the Common European Framework of Reference for Languages (CEFR) level A2 or above. The full list with explanations and examples of each grammar point can be found on the Chinese Grammar Wiki, the definitive source of information on Chinese grammar online.

CHAPTER 1	
Pronoun "mei" for "every"	每 + Measure Word (+ Noun)
Expressing "every" with "mei" and "dou"	每 ······ 都 ······
Measure words for counting	Number + Measure Word + Noun
Result complements "dao" and "jian"	Verb + 到 / 見
Expressing completion with "le"	Subj. + Verb + 了 + Obj.
Referring to "all" using "suoyou"	所 ······ 都 ······
Expressing experiences with "guo"	Verb + 過
"Zai" following verbs	Verb + 在 + Place
Modifying nouns with phrase + "de"	(Phrase) + 的 + Noun
Ordinal numbers with "di"	第 + Number (+ Measure Word)
Expressing "and also" with "hai"	還 + Verb
Basic comparisons with "yiyang"	Noun 1 + 跟 + Noun 2 + 一樣 + Adj.
"Already" with "yijing"	已經 ······ 了
In the future in general	以後, ······
Auxiliary verb "hui" for "will"	會 + Verb
"Before" in general	以前, ······

Expressing location with "zai...shang/xia/li"	在 + Location + 上/下/裡/旁邊
"Always" with "zongshi"	總是 + Verb.
Expressing lateness with "cai"	才
Two words for "but"	Statement, 可是/但是 + transitional statement
"Would like to" with "xiang"	想 + Verb
"All along" with "yizhi"	Subj. + 一直 + Predicate
At the time when	······的時候
After a specific time	Time/Time phrase + 以後
Expressing earliness with "jiu"	就
Modifying nouns with adjective + "de"	Adj. + 的 + Noun
Expressing "a little too" with "you dian"	有點 (兒) + Adj.
"Never" with "conglai"	從來不/從來沒 (有)
"Yinggai" for should	應該 / 該 + Verb
Explaining causes with "yinwei"	······，因為······
Using "zai" with verbs	Subj. + 在 + Place + Verb
Referring to "all" using "suoyou"	所有······都······
Causative verbs	Noun 1 + 讓/叫/請 + Noun 2······
Using "dui"	對 + Noun······
"If..., then..." with "ruguo..., jiu..."	如果······，就······
Expressing "with" with "gen"	跟······ + Verb
Expressing "together" with "yiqi"	一起 + Verb
Basic comparisons with "bi"	Noun 1 + 比 + Noun 2 + Adj.
"Not very" with "bu tai"	不太 + Adj.
Verbs with "gei"	Subj. + 給 + Target + Verb + Obj.
Doing something more with "duo"	多 + Verb
Measure words to differentiate	這 / 那 + Measure Word (+ Noun)

Result complement "-cuo"	Verb + 錯
"Just now" with "gangcai"	剛才 + Verb
"Even more" with "geng"	更 + Adj.
Using "ji" to mean "several"	幾 + Measure Word + Noun
Before a specific time	Time / Verb + 以前
Potential complement "bu dong"	Verb + 不動
"Just" with "jiu"	Subj. + 就 + (只) + Verb; 就 + single things or persons
Expressing duration with "le"	Verb + 了 + Duration

CHAPTER 5

Asking why with "zenme"	怎麼······?
Separable verb	Verb-Obj. / Verb + ... + Obj.
Negative commands with "bie"	別 + Verb

CHAPTER 6

"Both A and B" with "you"	又······又······
Expressing "in addition" with "haiyou"	Clause 1 ，還有 + (，)+ Clause 2
Sentence-final interjection "a"	······啊！
"Some" using "yixie"	一些 + Noun
Expressing "more and more" with "yue... yue..."	越······越······
"De" (modal particle)	······的

CHAPTER 7

Questions with "le ma"	Verb + 了 + 嗎？
Modifying nouns with adjective + "de"	Adj. + 的 + Noun
Indicating purpose or intent using "shi...de"	是······的

CHAPTER 8

There are no new grammar points in this chapter.

CHAPTER 9

Other Stories
from Mandarin Companion

Level 1 Readers: 300 Characters

The Secret Garden 《秘密花園》
by Frances Hodgson Burnett

Li Ye (Mary Lennox) grew up without the love and affection of her parents. After an epidemic leaves her an orphan, Li Ye is sent off to live with her reclusive uncle in his sprawling estate in Nanjing. She learns of a secret garden where no one has set foot in ten years. Li Ye finds the garden and slowly discovers the secrets of the manor. With the help of new friends, she brings the garden back to life and learns the healing power of friendship and love.

The Monkey's Paw 《猴爪》
by W. W. Jacobs

Mr. and Mrs. Zhang live with their grown son Guisheng who works at a factory. One day an old friend of Mr. Zhang comes to visit the family after having spent years traveling in the mysterious hills of China's Yunnan Province. He tells the Zhang family of a monkey's paw that has magical powers to grant three wishes to the holder. Against his better judgment, he reluctantly gives the monkey paw to the Zhang family, along with a warning that the wishes come with a great price for trying to change ones fate...

The Country of the Blind 《盲人國》
by H. G. Wells

"In the country of the blind, the one-eyed man is king" repeats in Chen Fangyuan's mind after he finds himself trapped in a valley holding a community of people for whom a disease eliminated their vision many generations before and no longer have a concept of sight. Chen Fangyuan quickly finds that these people have developed their other senses to compensate for their lack of sight. His insistence that he can see causes the entire community to believe he is crazy. With no way out, Chen Fangyuan begins to accept his fate until one day the village doctors believe they now understand what is the cause of his insanity… those useless round objects in his eye sockets.

Sherlock Holmes and the Case of the Curly-Haired Company 《卷髮公司的案子》
based on The Red Headed League by Sir Arthur Conan Doyle

Mr. Xie was recently hired by the Curly Haired Company. For a significant weekly allowance, he was required to sit in an office and copy articles from a book, while in the meantime his assistant looked after his shop. He had answered an advertisement in the paper and although hundreds of people applied, he was the only one selected because of his very curly hair. When the company unexpectedly closes, Mr. Xie visits Gao Ming (Sherlock Holmes) with his strange story. Gao Ming is certain something is not right, but will he solve the mystery in time?

The Prince and the Pauper 《王子和穷孩子》
by Mark Twain

During a chance encounter, two nearly identical boys, one a poor beggar and the other a prince, decide to exchange places. The pauper, now living in the royal palace, is constantly filled with the dread of being discovered for who and what he really is while the Prince, dressed in rags, lives on the street enduring hardships he never thought possible. Both children soon discover that neither life is as carefree as they expected.

Level 2 Readers: 450 Characters

Great Expectations: Part 1 《美好的前途（上）》
by Charles Dickens

Great Expectations is hailed as Charles Dickens' masterpiece. A gripping tale of love and loss, aspiration and moral redemption, the story follows the young orphan Xiaomao (Pip) from poverty to a life of unexpected opportunity and wealth. In Part 1, Xiaomao is raised by his short-tempered older sister and her husband who run a small repair shop in the outskirts of Shanghai. Xiaomao dreams of leaving his life of poverty behind after becoming playmates with the beautiful Bingbing (Estella), daughter of the eccentric Bai Xiaojie (Ms. Havisham). His prospects for the future are bleak, until one day a mysterious benefactor gives Xiaomao the opportunity of a lifetime.

Great Expectations: Part 2 《美好的前途（下）》
by Charles Dickens

Great Expectations is hailed as Charles Dickens' masterpiece. A gripping tale of love and loss, aspiration and moral redemption, the story follows the young orphan Xiaomao (Pip) from poverty to a life of unexpected opportunity and wealth. In Part 2, Xiaomao leaves his life of poverty behind to seek his fortunes in Shanghai and win the heart of the beautiful yet cold-hearted Bingbing (Estella). Xiaomao's world is turned upside down when his mysterious benefactor is revealed and his deepest secrets are brought into the light of day.

Journey to the Center of the Earth 《地心遊記》
by Jules Verne

Join Professor Luo and his niece Xiaojing in their daring quest down the mouth of a volcano to reach the center of the earth. Guided by a mysterious passage on an ancient parchment and accompanied by their faithful guide Lao Xu, the three explorers encounter subterranean phenomenon, prehistoric animals, and vast underground seas. "A Journey to the Center of the Earth" is one of Jules Verne's best-known works and one of the most classic tales of adventure ever written.

Mandarin Companion is producing a growing library of graded readers for Chinese language learners.

Visit our website for the newest books available:

www.MandarinCompanion.com

CPSIA information can be obtained
at www.ICGtesting.com
Printed in the USA
BVHW011015030621
608728BV00005B/179